FOLK TALES FROM ASIA
FOR CHILDREN EVERYWHERE

Book Two

sponsored by the
Asian Cultural Centre for Unesco

New York · WEATHERHILL/HEIBONSHA · *Tokyo*

This is the second volume of Asian folk tales to be published under the Asian Copublication Programme carried out, in cooperation with Unesco, by the Asian Cultural Centre for Unesco / Tokyo Book Development Centre. As explained in the Editors' Note that concluded the first volume, the stories have been selected and, with the editorial help of Miss Eileen Colwell of England, edited by a five-country central editorial board in consultation with the Unesco member states in Asia.

First edition, 1975

Jointly published by John Weatherhill, Inc., 149 Madison Avenue, New York, New York 10016, with editorial offices at 7-6-13 Roppongi, Minato-ku, Tokyo; and Heibonsha, Tokyo. Copyright © 1975 by the Asian Cultural Centre for Unesco / Tokyo Book Development Centre, 6 Fukuro-machi, Shinjuku-ku, Tokyo. Printed in Japan.

LIBRARY OF CONGRESS CATALOGING IN PUBLICATION DATA: Main entry under title: Folk tales from Asia for children everywhere / "Sponsored by the Asian Cultural Centre for Unesco" / SUMMARY: A two-volume collection of traditional folk tales from various Asian countries illustrated by native artists / [1. Folklore—Asia] / I. Yunesuko Ajia Bunka Sentā / PZ8.1.F717 / 398.2'095 [E] / 74-82605 / ISBN 0-8348-1032-8 (v. 1).   ISBN 0-8348-1033-6 (v. 2)

Contents

The Story of Rice

Once Batara Guru, the Lord of Gods, was building himself a new palace, and he sent word to all the gods in heaven that each must bring a big stone for the foundation of the palace. Everyone promised to obey the command except the Snake God. When the Messenger God came to him, the Snake God shook his head sadly and said: "As you can see, I have neither arms nor legs. How could I carry a stone?" As he spoke, three large teardrops rolled down his cheeks. When the teardrops fell to the ground, they turned into three white eggs. "Take those eggs to the Lord of Gods and tell him exactly what happened," the Messenger God told the Snake God.

So the Snake God set off for the royal palace holding the three eggs carefully in his mouth. On his way he met the Great Eagle. "Where are you going, Snake God?" asked the Great Eagle. But

the Snake God's mouth was so full of eggs that he could not answer. The Great Eagle repeated his question twice more and, getting no answer, became very angry. He started pecking the Snake God on the head. This hurt so much that the Snake God gave two loud cries, and each time he opened his mouth one of the eggs fell out.

As the eggs hit the ground, they broke open and out of each came a piglet. The two piglets were adopted by a cow and raised together with her own calf. The calf's name was Lembu Gumarang, and as we shall see, he grew up to be an evil bull with magical powers, a great enemy of both gods and men.

The Snake God was sorry he had lost the two eggs, but by good luck one still remained safe in his mouth. He brought this last egg to the Lord of Gods and told him what had happened. The Lord of Gods ordered him to keep the egg until it hatched and then to bring him whatever came out of it.

The Snake God carried the egg home and took very good care of it. Finally, at the end of a month, the egg broke open and out of it came a beautiful baby girl. The Snake God hurried to take the baby to the Lord of Gods, who adopted the baby as his own daughter and named her Dewi Sri. She was brought up as a princess in the royal palace with all the loving care that a daughter of the Lord of Gods should have.

As the years passed, Dewi Sri grew up to be a lovely young lady. She was as gentle and kindhearted as she was beautiful, and everyone who knew her loved her. The Lord of Gods himself showed her so much affection that the other gods began to fear he might want to marry her. The law said that no father could marry his daughter, not even if he was a god and she was only his adopted daughter. The gods feared that if this law was broken, the whole kingdom would be ruined. So they met secretly and

decided that Dewi Sri must be killed. This decision filled them with sadness, but they thought this was the only way to save the kingdom.

So the gods put poison in a piece of Dewi Sri's favorite fruit and gave it to her. No sooner had she eaten the fruit than she fell sick. Day by day she grew weaker and weaker, and finally she died. It was just as though the slender stalk of a young flower had gradually wilted and fallen to the ground. Dewi Sri's body was buried with royal ceremony, just beside a beautiful triple-roofed pagoda, and a royal servant was left to guard the grave and to water it daily so that flowers would grow around it.

Presently from the grave there appeared a strange kind of plant that no one had ever seen before. This was the heavenly plant now called rice. Rapidly it grew tall and put out many ears, which in time turned yellow and produced many grains of rice.

When the Lord of Gods saw this miracle, he told the royal servant to take the rice seeds down to earth and give them to the king of the land called Pajajaran. "Tell the king," he said, "that the seeds are a gift from me. Let his people plant them and take good care of them, and then no one need ever go hungry again, for rice is the food of life."

The king of Pajajaran was very happy to receive this wonderful gift from heaven. He distributed the rice among his people. The royal servant from heaven taught the people how to sow the seed both in paddy fields and on hillside terraces, how to harvest the plants, and how to thresh the rice. Then a goddess from heaven came down to earth and taught all the young girls how to cook the rice and serve it in many delicious ways. After that time the people of Pajajaran never lacked food. For many years they lived in peace and happiness.

But one day a wicked merchant from another land came to Pajajaran to trade. Seeing and tasting the wonderful rice, he wanted to buy it all and take it away, but the king refused, saying: "This rice doesn't really belong to us but to heaven, for it came from the grave of the heavenly Dewi Sri. So we cannot sell it to you." This made the merchant very angry. He went to the cave of the calf Lembu Gumarang, now grown into an evil bull with magical powers, and asked him to destroy all the rice in Pajajaran.

The bull set to work at once. He blew up a great wind that crushed all the growing rice plants to the ground. Seeing this, the Lord of Gods sent a young god named Sulanjana to save the rice. Sulanjana blew away the wind and lifted the young plants upright again.

Then the evil bull called his foster brothers to help him destroy the rice. These were the two piglets, now grown to be huge, fierce hogs. There was a terrible fight between the animals and the god Sulanjana. The animals called up hundreds of wild pigs to trample the rice, but the god filled the land with such heavy fog that all the pigs lost their way. Then they sent thousands of rats to nibble the rice plants, but the god set poison in their tracks so that all the rats fell dead. Again the wicked brothers called millions of birds to peck the ears of the rice, but the god frightened the birds away with his magic spells.

At last the evil bull called all the wild beasts in the forest and told them to destroy all the towns and villages of the country. Then all the people, even the young children, came to fight beside the god. Under his leadership they dug holes and set traps in them and they fastened nets to the treetops.

Suddenly the army of wild beasts, led by the bull, came rushing from the forests, crashing through the trees. But many of them fell into the traps and many more were caught in the nets. The bull saw that his army was losing, but still he would not surrender. "Sulanjana," he called to the god, "don't think I've lost yet. I dare you to come fight with me and see who is the stronger."

The young god stepped out bravely to meet the challenge. He stood with his hands on his hips, waiting for the bull to charge. The bull sharpened his horns against a tree trunk and then came rushing at Sulanjana with all his terrible force. But the young god jumped aside at the last minute; and as the bull went charging by, the god stuck out one foot and tripped the bull so that he came crashing to the ground. Quickly the bull rose to his feet and charged again, only to be tripped once more. Again and again the bull charged, but each time Sulanjana was too quick for him.

At last the god grabbed one of the bull's feet and swung the animal round and round in the air. Finally the bull could not stand it anymore. He cried out for mercy, and the god agreed to spare his life if he and the two evil hogs would promise to guard the rice fields forever after.

The animals promised and the people of Pajajaran cheered. From that time on the rice fields have been loyally guarded by the animals, and the fields have never been disturbed again. And ever since that time the people of Pajajaran have lived in peace and happiness, enjoying the delicious rice that is the food of life.

Retold and translated by Ati K. Kartahadimadja
Illustrated by A. Wakjan

The Picture Wife

Once upon a time there was a man whose name was Gombei. He was poor and rather weak in the head. He lived in a hut all by himself. No one would marry him because he was so simple-minded.

Then one evening a young woman came to his door and asked if she could spend the night in his hut. Such a beautiful woman Gombei had never seen before and he was only too glad to let her in. That night after supper, the young woman said: "It seems that you live here alone. I am alone too. Would you like me for yout wife?"

Gombei couldn't believe his good fortune! And so they were married.

Gombei's marriage made him very happy, but it also made it very difficult for him to get his work done. He was so fond of his young wife that he could not bear to turn his eyes away from her, not even for a moment. When he made straw sandals, they often became five or six feet long before he noticed, for he kept his eyes on his wife and not on his work. When he made straw raincoats, they were sometimes ten or twenty feet long, for he watched to see what his wife was doing instead of paying attention to what he was doing himself. No one could wear his sandals or his raincoats.

Then he went into the fields to work. Every few minutes he came running home, shouting: "Are you there, dear wife?" So he did not accomplish much in a day.

"This simply won't do!" said his wife. So she went to the town and asked an artist to paint her portrait. She took it home and told

Gombei: "Here is my picture. Hang it on the nearest mulberry tree. If you can see it while you are working in the fields, you won't miss me so much."

Gombei did as he was told. Every few minutes he stopped work to look at his wife's portrait, but he no longer ran home so often. One day, however, a sudden gust of wind caught the picture and blew it up into the sky. Gombei tried to catch it, but soon it was out of sight. Crying bitterly, Gombei ran home to tell his wife. "Never mind, dear husband," she comforted him. "I will go to town and have another picture painted for you."

In the meantime the first picture had gone on floating along in the air until it finally came fluttering down in the garden of a castle. When the lord of the castle saw it, he immediately fell in love with the woman in the picture. "If there is a portrait, there must be a person," he thought, and he ordered his men to find the woman and bring her to him without delay.

The men went from village to village with the picture, asking if anyone knew the woman. At last they came to the village where Gombei lived. "Do you know this woman?" they asked the villagers, showing them the picture.

"Oh, that's Gombei's wife," replied the villagers as soon as they saw the picture.

Sure enough, when the men went to Gombei's hut, there they found a beautiful woman who looked exactly like the one in the portrait.

"We'll take her to our lord," they said and tried to carry her off.

"Please don't take her away," begged Gombei, but all his begging was in vain. He cried so much that his tears made a pool a foot across.

"Don't cry so, Gombei," said his wife. "We can do nothing

now, but listen carefully. You must come to the castle on New Year's Eve. Bring pine trees for the New Year gate decorations when you come. Then we'll be able to see each other again and all will be well."

Before she could say anything more, she was taken away to the castle. Every day Gombei wondered if it was time to go yet. At last someone told him that it was New Year's Eve. He started for the castle with a huge bundle of pine trees on his back. He would soon see his dear wife again!

When he reached the castle gates, he shouted: "Pine trees, pine trees! Fine pine trees for the New Year!"

Inside the castle, his wife heard him and smiled. It was the first time she had smiled since she was brought into the castle. The lord was so pleased to see her cheerful that he ordered his servants to call the pine-seller in.

When Gombei appeared, his wife looked even more cheerful. She beamed at him with such delight that the lord thought to himself: "If a pine-seller can please her so much, I will become one myself."

He ordered Gombei to change clothes with him. Dressed shabbily as a pine-seller, he walked up and down in the garden shouting: "Pine trees, pine trees! Fine pine trees for the New Year!"

This made Gombei's wife even more pleased. She clapped her little hands and laughed heartily. The lord was so delighted to see her laugh that he danced about in the garden with the pine trees on his back. "Pine trees, fine pine trees!" he shouted again and again. Round and round the garden he danced, and out of the castle gates he went without even noticing.

As soon as he was outside, Gombei's wife told the servants to shut the gates of the castle. After a while, the lord realized that he was no longer in the garden. He went up to the castle gates

and to his astonishment he found them closed. "Let me in! Let me in!" he shouted, but no one answered.

Within the castle Gombei and his clever wife now had everything they could wish for and lived happily ever after.

Retold by Keigo Seki
Translated by Kyoko Matsuoka
Illustrated by Toshio Kajiyama

The Four Bald Men

Once there was a man who earned his living by making baskets out of palm leaves. One day he climbed to the top of a tall palm tree to gather leaves and weave baskets.

As he sat there working and whistling merrily, he thought to himself: "I ought to have a servant to do this for me! I'll sell this basket for a high price when I finish it. Then I'll make more and more baskets until I've saved enough to hire a servant."

Pleased at the thought of having a servant to work for him, he said: "And if he doesn't work hard, I'll kick him out—like this!" Forgetting where he was, he lifted one leg and kicked so hard that he lost his balance and fell from the top of the tree.

It was only by good luck that he managed to catch hold of some palm leaves and hang from them by his hands, shouting: "Help! Help!"

At that moment an elephant-driver came by riding an elephant. Hearing a cry for help coming from the sky, he looked up and saw the basket-maker hanging from the tree.

"Get me down!" shouted the basket-maker, "and I promise to be your servant for the rest of my life."

At once the elephant-driver guided his elephant to the tree. Standing on its back, he reached up and caught hold of the basket-maker's feet.

Just at that moment the elephant, feeling the driver's feet pressing hard on its back, thought this was the sign to move ahead. So it walked away, leaving the basket-maker hanging from the palm leaves and the elephant-driver hanging from the basket-maker's legs.

Now both men began to shout: "Help! Help!" It so happened that four bald men were passing by. Hearing the cries for help, they stopped in surprise.

"Save us! Save us!" cried the basket-maker and the elephant-driver. "We promise to be your servants for the rest of our lives."

The four bald men were pleased to think that they would get

two servants so easily. "Hold on!" they shouted and ran to get a net. Then they tied the corners of the net around their necks and held the net under the tree and cried: "Let go and drop! We'll catch you!"

At once the basket-maker let go of the palm leaves and he and the elephant-driver fell right into the middle of the net.

The shock was so great that the four bald men were jerked together. Their bald heads cracked against each other with such force that they all fell dead right then and there.

But the basket-maker and the elephant-driver walked away quite unhurt, chatting together cheerfully.

Retold by Ken Kun
Translated by Hong Them
Illustrated by Huot Thun

20

The Adventures of King Suton

Long, long ago there was a peaceful and prosperous kingdom called Mambang Negara. The king, Raja Suton, was an able and just ruler and his queen, Puteri Ikadon, was beautiful.

One day the queen had a longing to eat deer meat; so the king ordered a hunter, Tok Pawang, to search for a deer in the forest. As he was hiding in a thicket of bushes beside a pool, watching for deer, he saw seven beautiful princesses from the heavenly kingdom of Kayangan alight beside the water and bathe in the pool. Each left her wings upon the bank.

The youngest princess, Cempaka Biru, was so beautiful that Tok Pawang resolved to capture her as a gift for the king. He hid her wings, and when her sisters flew away, Cempaka Biru could not follow them. She begged Tok Pawang to give her back her wings, but he would not. He made her promise to obey him. Then he took her to the king, who married her as his second wife, as was the custom. Tok Pawang also gave her wings to King Suton, who locked them away in a chest.

After a time the queen became jealous of Cempaka Biru, for the king paid her more attention than he paid the queen herself. She complained bitterly to her parents, and her father, angry at the slight to his daughter, sent the king a false dream. He thought that if he could send the king away from the palace, he and his daughter the queen could get rid of Cempaka Biru while he was away. So the king dreamed one night that he must search for a white elephant with black tusks as a gift for Cempaka Biru, and the next morning he set off to look for it.

As soon as the king had left the palace, the queen ordered Cempaka Biru to dance. "I could dance much better if I had my wings," said Cempaka Biru, and the queen brought them from the king's chest. Cempaka Biru put on the wings, and suddenly, in the middle of the dance, she flew away, for she knew that her life was in danger. However, she did not return at once to her home in Kayangan but hid and waited for King Suton to pass that way.

Before long the king rode along the path, for he had soon decided that he had been tricked and he was anxious to see what had happened to Cempaka Biru in his absence. To his astonishment, Cempaka Biru appeared before him and told him of the plot against her life. "I dare not go back," she said. "Take this magic ring, for if you decide to follow me to Kayangan, you will need it to pass the Splitting Rock and the terrible bird the Roc. Show them this ring and repeat my name and they will spare you."

Weeping, Cempaka Biru bade the king farewell and he returned sadly to the palace. He found to his horror that his queen had indeed planned to kill Cempaka Biru. He did not delay a moment but set out at once to follow his princess to Kayangan.

When he was still miles away he could hear the crashing of the Splitting Rock. It was a terrifying sight, for every moment it opened and shut with a grinding roar. There was no room even for a fly between the two halves of the rock. The king showed Cempaka Biru's ring and spoke her name and at once the rock was still. In the silence the king passed through it unharmed.

Next King Suton came to the Roc, a gigantic bird with a sharp curved beak and glittering eyes. "How dare you come here, you puny human being!" screeched the Roc. "I shall devour you for my dinner!" But King Suton showed the Roc the magic ring and

spoke the princess's name, and the bird agreed to spare him and
to carry him to Kayangan.

In Kayangan, King Suton disguised himself as old man called
Awang Hitam, for he did not want the king of Kayangan to know
who he was until he had found the princess Cempaka Biru.

One day King Suton was walking near the palace gates, hoping
to catch a glimpse of his wife, when he saw many women with
water jugs on their heads going into the palace carrying water for
Cempaka Biru's bath. Quickly he climbed a tree close to the
palace gates and, as the women passed beneath its branches, he
leaned down and dropped the magic ring into one of the water
jugs. Cempaka Biru recognized it at once. "My husband, King
Suton, must have reached Kayangan," she thought with joy. But

although she inquired everywhere, she could not hear of anyone like King Suton being in the kingdom, and she became ill with sorrow. The king her father summoned all the witch doctors in Kayangan to his daughter, but no one could cure her.

At last the king of Kayangan was told that there was a wizard called Awang Hitam in the country who had some skill. He was summoned to the palace and so at last King Suton and Cempaka Biru were together again. As soon as she saw her husband she was cured of her illness.

King Suton asked her father's permission to take Cempaka Biru back to earth as his wife, but her father insisted that first King Suton must prove that he was worthy of a princess of Kayangan. "First clear away the thick forest," he commanded, "and then I shall believe that you are a wizard."

King Suton sat and thought deeply of the magical powers of his ancestors, and the God of the Seventh Heaven knew what he was thinking and sent him help.

Elephants by the thousand came and uprooted all the trees until there was not one left standing. "Your Majesty, the task is done," said King Suton.

"Now you must burn the trees without using fire," said the king of Kayangan.

King Suton sat and thought deeply of the magical powers of his ancestors, and the God of the Seventh Heaven sent him thousands of magic birds with fiery beaks and all the trees were burned. "Your Majesty, the task is done," said King Suton.

Now the king of Kayangan scattered three sacks of sesame seeds on the ground and ordered King Suton to pick them all up, missing not one. King Suton sat and thought deeply of the magical powers of his ancestors, and the God of the Seventh Heaven sent many birds-of-paradise, who picked up the seeds until the three sacks were as full as they were to begin with. Not one single seed had they missed. "Your Majesty, the task is done," said King Suton.

"I will set you one last task," said the king of Kayangan. He showed King Suton seven booths, each one like the other. "In each of these," said the king of Kayangan, "is one of my seven daughters. Each will stick her forefinger out through this small hole in the door. You must say which is Cempaka Biru's finger. If you decide correctly, you may take her away. If not, you shall die!"

Once again King Suton sat and thought deeply of the magical powers of his ancestors, and the God of the Seventh Heaven sent a green fly to buzz round his head. King Suton watched it as it flew along the line of booths. It settled on the forefinger of the princess in the middle booth. "This is Cempaka Biru's finger!" cried King Suton.

At last the king of Kayangan was satisfied. "Truly you are

worthy of my daughter," he agreed. "You are indeed a wizard able to do impossible things!"

He ordered a magnificent banquet to be prepared and in the sight of all the people of Kayangan, King Suton and Cempaka Biru were married again, this time according to the customs of Kayangan. Then King Suton cast off his disguise and he and Cempaka Biru returned to his kingdom on earth. There they lived happily ever after.

Retold by Saleh Daud
Translated by Hamsiah Abdul Hamid
Illustrated by Meor Shariman Hassan

The Old Woman in the Gourd

Long, long ago an old woman set out to visit her married daughter who had gone to live some distance away.

By and by she came to a thick forest and there she met a fox. "Old woman, I have been without food for ten days," said the fox. "You can go no farther, for I shall eat you up!"

"Be patient, dear fox," said the old woman. "I am going to see my daughter, but in a month I shall be coming back this way, so please let me go. I am thin now, but then I shall be fat and you can eat me as soon as you like."

"A fat woman would make a better meal than a thin one," thought the fox, so he let her go. She hurried away, hoping that no one else would try to stop her.

She had not gone far when the ferocious king of the forest, the tiger, appeared and snarled: "Old woman, I have been hungry for twenty days. You will make a meal for me—be prepared to die!"

"Please let me go, O King of Beasts," said the old woman. "You can eat me when I come back from visiting my daughter at the end of a month. By then I'll be fat and tasty, not thin and tough as I am now."

So the tiger let her go.

Before long the King of Monkeys, with all his tribe, stood in her way. To deceive her, he greeted her politely with a garland of sweet-smelling flowers. Then he said with a grin: "Old woman, you have come just in time. I shall have pleasure in eating you."

"Be patient, O Lord of Monkeys," said the old woman. "I

am on my way to visit my daughter, so please let me go. I am thin now, but in a month I'll be fat and then you can eat me as soon as you like."

But the King of Monkeys was not as easily tricked as the fox and the tiger. At his command a regiment of monkeys surrounded her, shrieking and screaming. The little ones even dared to climb up onto her shoulders and jump on her head.

She begged and prayed them to let her go, but the King of Monkeys said: "I shall not believe you are really coming back this way unless you swear by the Buddha!"

The old woman had to take the oath, and then she was allowed to go on her way. At long last she reached her daughter's house and stayed there happily. But the time flew by and the end of the month came all too soon. Then she remembered her promise to the animals and told her daughter all about it. They put their heads together and made a plan. The daughter brought two big gourds. One was a Lanka, which is shaped like a bottle, and the other was a Chinda, shaped like a snake. The daughter put the old woman inside the Lanka and asked the Chinda to lead the way. Thus they came into the forest where the monkeys, the tiger, and the fox were waiting hungrily for the old woman.

At the crossroads the monkeys were

gathered, growing more suspicious every moment. Suddenly they heard a strange rattling sound and saw the Chinda approaching, followed by the big Lanka.

"Make way for us!" called the Chinda loudly. "What do you mean by blocking our way like this!"

Taken aback by this unexpected challenge, the King of Monkeys said politely: "We were just waiting for an old woman who has promised to be our dinner. As you came along did you see her by any chance?"

"What business have we with your old woman?" said the Chinda haughtily. "Out of our way!" And the Chinda and the Lanka rattled on.

Soon they came to the place where the tiger was waiting. He was determined not to listen to a single word from the old woman this time but to pounce on her and gobble her up at once.

First there came a strange sound and then the tiger saw the Chinda rolling toward him followed by the rocking Lanka.

"Make way for us!" shouted the Chinda.

Bewildered, the tiger stepped out of the way; then suddenly remembering, he said: "Oh, have you seen the old woman who promised to be my dinner?"

"What business have we with your old woman?" said the Chinda. "Out of our way!" And the Chinda and the Lanka passed on.

By this time the fox had heard about the strange carriage that was rolling through the forest and he was very suspicious. So he placed a sharp-edged stone in the middle of the pathway. Then he hid behind a tree and waited.

By and by, here came the Chinda and the Lanka at great speed. The old woman was chuckling to herself at the clever way they had tricked the monkeys and the tiger.

"Crack!" The Lanka hit the sharp stone and split from top to bottom, throwing the old woman onto the path.

Now, the monkeys and the tiger had soon realized the trick that had been played on them and were pursuing the Lanka. Just as the fox was about to eat the old woman all by himself, the other animals came racing up.

The old woman knew that she was caught this time, but she hadn't given up hope yet. She agreed that the animals should eat her, but said: "It would be wise to roast me first. I shall taste better that way."

So the animals made a fire to roast her. "The fire must turn to ashes before it is ready; then I shall be cooked in no time," said the old woman, hoping to delay them still further.

When at last the fire turned to ashes, the old woman took a stone and sat on it in the middle of the heap. The animals, thinking their meal would soon be ready, closed their eyes and made their customary prayer.

Quickly the old woman scooped up some ashes and threw them in the animals' faces so that they were blinded. Before they could recover, she ran out of the forest and escaped.

Furiously angry and very hungry, the fox, the tiger, and the King of Monkeys searched everywhere for the old woman. But they never saw her again.

Retold by Madhav Lal Karmacharya
Translated by M. L. Karmacharya
Illustrated by Tek Bir Mukhiya

The Farmer's Wife and the Tiger

One day a farmer went with his oxen to plow his field. He had just turned the first furrow when a tiger walked up and said: "Peace be with you, friend. How are you this fine morning?"

"The same to you, my lord, and I am pretty well, thank you," replied the farmer, quaking with fear but thinking it wisest to be polite.

"I am glad to hear it, because Heaven has sent me to eat your two oxen," said the tiger cheerfully. "You are a God-fearing man, I know, so make haste and unyoke them."

"Aren't you making a mistake, my lord?" asked the farmer. His courage had returned now that he knew the tiger was only proposing to gobble up his oxen, not him. "Heaven sent me to plow this field, and in order to do so, I must have oxen. Hadn't you better go and make further inquiries?"

"There is no need to delay, and I should be sorry to keep you waiting," said the tiger. "If you'll unyoke the oxen, I'll be ready in a moment to eat them." With that the tiger began to sharpen his teeth and claws in a very frightening manner.

The farmer begged and prayed that his oxen might not be eaten and promised that, if the tiger would spare them, he would give in exchange a fine fat young milk cow of his wife's.

To this the tiger agreed, and taking the oxen with him for safety, the farmer hurried home. Seeing him return so early from the fields, his wife, who was an energetic, hard-working woman, called out: "What! Lazy bones! Back already and my work just beginning!"

The farmer explained how he had met the tiger and how, to save his oxen, he had promised the cow in exchange. At this his wife began to shout, saying: "A likely story indeed! What do you mean by saving your stupid oxen at the expense of my beautiful cow! Where will the children get milk? How can I cook without butter?"

"All very fine, wife," retorted the farmer, "but how can we make bread without grain? How can we have grain without oxen to plow the fields? It's surely better to do without milk and butter than without bread. So make haste and untie the cow."

"You great silly!" scolded his wife. "If you had an ounce of sense in your brain, you'd think of some plan to get us out of our difficulty!"

"Think of one yourself!" cried her husband in a rage.

"So I will!" replied his wife. "But if I do the thinking, you must obey me, for I can't do both. Go

35

back to the tiger and tell him that the cow wouldn't come with you, but that your wife is bringing it."

The farmer, who was a great coward, didn't like the idea of going back empty-handed to the tiger, but as he could not think of any other plan, he did as he was told. He found the tiger still sharpening his claws and teeth, he was so hungry. When he heard that he had to wait still longer for his dinner, he began to growl and lash his tail and curl his whiskers in a most terrible manner causing the poor farmer's knees to knock together with terror.

Now, when the farmer had left the house, his wife went out to the stable and saddled the pony. Then she put on her husband's best clothes, tied the turban high so as to look as tall as possible, jumped astride the pony, and set off to the field where the tiger was waiting.

She rode along, swaggering like a man, till she came to where the lane turned into the field, and there she called out as bold as brass: "Now, please the powers I may find a tiger in the field! I haven't tasted tiger since yesterday when I ate three for breakfast."

Hearing these words and seeing the speaker ride boldly toward him, the tiger was so alarmed that he turned tail and bolted into the forest. He went at such a headlong pace that he nearly knocked down his own jackal—tigers always have a jackal of their own to clear away the bones after they have finished eating.

"My lord! My lord!" cried the jackal. "Where are you going so fast?"

"Run! Run!" panted the tiger. "There's the very devil of a horseman in yonder field who thinks nothing of eating three tigers for breakfast!"

At this the jackal laughed behind his paw. "My dear master," he said, "the sun has dazzled your eyes! That was no horseman, but only the farmer's wife dressed up as a man!"

"Are you quite sure?" asked the tiger, pausing in his flight.

"Quite sure, my lord," said the jackal, "and if your lordship's eyes had not been dazzled—ahem—by the sun, your lordship would have seen the woman's pigtail hanging down behind her."

"But you may be mistaken," persisted the cowardly tiger. "She was the very devil of a horseman to look at!"

"Who's afraid!" replied the jackal. "Come! Don't give up your dinner because of a woman! We'll go together."

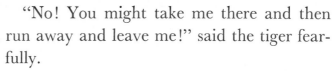

"No! You might take me there and then run away and leave me!" said the tiger fearfully.

"Well, let us tie our tails together then, so that I can't!" suggested the cunning jackal. He was determined not to be done out of his bones at the end of the feast.

To this the tiger agreed, and having tied their tails together in a reef knot, the pair set off arm in arm.

Now the farmer and his wife had remained in the field, laughing over the trick they had played on the tiger. Suddenly, lo and behold, what should they see but the tiger and the jackal coming toward them with their tails tied together.

"Run!" cried the farmer. "We are lost! We are lost!"

"Nothing of the kind, you great baby," answered his wife coolly. "Stop that noise! I can't hear myself speak!"

She waited until the pair of animals was within hail, then called out politely: "How very kind of you, dear Mr. Jackal, to bring me such a nice fat tiger! I shan't be a moment finishing off my share of him, and then you can have the bones."

At these words the tiger became wild with fright and, quite forgetting the jackal and the reef knot in their tails, he bolted away full tilt, dragging the jackal behind him. Bumpety, bump, bump, over the stones! Scritch, scratch, scramble, through the thorny bushes!

In vain the poor jackal howled and shrieked to the tiger to stop, but the noise behind him only frightened the coward more. Away he went, helter-skelter, hurry-scurry, over hill and dale, till he was nearly dead with fatigue, and the jackal was *quite* dead from bumps and bruises.

And the farmer and his wife were never troubled by the tiger again.

Retold by Ikram Chughtai
Translated by Ikram Chunghtai
and S. Afaq Ahmed
Illustrated by Naheed Jafri

The Fisherman's Daughter

Lingayen Gulf in Pangasinian Province is very beautiful but beneath its shimmering beauty lies danger. In the gulf there is a whirlpool that can suddenly suck the bodies of swimmers into its depths. Every year someone, often a young girl, is drowned in this whirlpool. It is said that the god of the gulf has demanded a life each year, ever since the daughter of a fisherman refused to stay with him. This is how the story goes.

Long ago, before the Spaniards came to rule over the Philippines, there lived a poor fisherman, his wife, and their only child. The child was so happy and cheerful that her parents named her Maliket. Although she was small, she was nimble and strong. In the early mornings when her parents woke up, they would find their breakfast of fried fish, boiled rice, and a hot drink made from ground rice already prepared.

"What would we do without her?" her old parents asked each other as they watched their daughter cooking meals and washing clothes. It was a pleasure to them also to see her enjoyment as she raced with the wind along the shore. What she loved most, however, was to sail out to sea in her sturdy wooden banca. She liked to search for hidden coves and to explore lonely caves.

One evening she came home with a strange kind of seaweed. "Where in the world did you find this?" asked her mother.

"I've discovered a wonderful cove to bathe in. I think I must be the first person to set foot in it. It's at the foot of that mountain," said Maliket, pointing to a steep rocky mountain in the distance.

40

"That is an evil place, my child!" said her father in alarm. "It is said that Maksil, the god of this gulf, loves to take his nap there. He punishes any mortal who dares disturb his peace. Promise me never to go there again."

Maliket laughed. "Father, there is no god there, only strange fish and birds. But if you don't want me to go, I promise not to."

Now Maksil, the god of the gulf, had seen Maliket bathing in his cove. He had just lost his only daughter, so he wanted Maliket to take her place. "She reminds me so much of my dear child," he said. He called his servant Giant Squid to him and ordered him to steer Maliket's banca to his cove when next she put to sea.

So the next time she took her banca out, Maliket found herself drifting toward the hidden cove. Not wanting to break her promise to her father she tried to alter her course, but it was in vain.

Soon her banca was in the cove and was being drawn under the water into a deep tunnel-like passage. At first she was a little frightened, but she soon forgot her fear, for there were such wonderful sights around her. On both banks were fragrant flowers of many different colors, and tall trees heavy with shining fruit. Below her in the clear water were fish of many shapes, sizes, and colors. They were talking and laughing, and, strangely enough, Maliket understood them.

"Welcome, Maliket!" they cried. "Welcome to our master's kingdom. Stay with us and be happy forever."

She stretched out her hands to them, but suddenly there was a loud sound like the crack of a whip and all the fishes disappeared. Terrified, she seized her paddle, but before she could use it, her banca struck the shore and she was thrown out onto soft mossy ground.

When she looked up she saw a tall bronze figure, half-human, half-fish. He was sitting on a throne, wearing a shining crown and

holding a magnificent silver sceptre, shaped like an eel. "Don't be afraid, Maliket," the strange being said in a booming voice. "I am Maksil, god of the gulf. I have brought you here to take my dear daughter's place. You shall have everything you wish."

"But my parents will miss me!" wailed Maliket. "Please, please, let me go home."

"That is impossible!" Maksil roared, and the ground beneath the sea trembled at his fury. Then, seeing the girl's terror, he changed his tone and spoke more gently. "When you have been here longer, you will forget your poor ugly home. You see that silver palace," and he waved his hands toward a beautiful building glittering with precious stones, "that will be your home. You will have servants and playmates at your command, jewels and fine clothes to wear, and delicious food to eat. Come with me, child."

But Maliket refused to obey him. So Maksil clapped his hands and two servants picked her up and carried her forcibly into the palace. Mermaids came from every direction. They bathed her and dressed her in a silver gown. One placed a flower-shaped

crown of pearls on her head. Others brought her the loveliest jewels from the deepest caverns of the sea. But Maliket was not interested in any of these beautiful things. She only said, weeping: "Please ask your master to send me home. My parents are old and need my help."

The god of Lingayen Gulf had never before been disobeyed and he was more determined than ever to make her stay with him. He called on his best entertainers to amuse her. Child that she was, Maliket forgot her homesickness for a while as she saw fish clowns, jugglers, and circus performers do their acts. Handsome little boys and pretty girls—half-human, half-fish like their master—taught her to play their sea games. Maksil was happy to hear her laughter.

"The little one is beginning to like her new home," he remarked. But he was mistaken. Soon Maliket's homesickness returned. She had found a small magic mirror on a dusty shelf and in it she saw her sick mother and her old father anxiously searching for her.

Her nurse, Akulaw, a human being like herself, found Maliket weeping pitifully and said: "Do you really wish to go home, child?"

"Oh, yes, I do, I do!"

"I understand how you feel, for like you I was brought here by force. I was young then. Now I am an old woman and I have never seen my family again."

"Oh, please, help me to go home," pleaded Maliket. "Won't you come with me too?"

"No, I am too old now, but I should like you to give me your magic mirror so that I could always see what was going on in the human world—and also see what happens to you, child. Now, listen! Tonight I will come for you and help you escape from the palace. I will do all I can, but once you are on the open sea, you will have to manage by yourself."

That night Akulaw put a sleeping powder in Giant Squid's drink. Then she led Maliket out of the palace by secret ways to

the place where her banca was hidden. There one of Akulaw's trusty friends met them and helped Maliket to paddle her banca through the underwater tunnel to the open sea. Then he left her and Maliket set out for home.

When Maksil discovered that Maliket had gone, he ordered Giant Squid to bring her back. Squid did his best but he could not swim as fast as usual because of the sleeping powder. Maliket saw him coming and paddled with all her strength. She was so near the shore that her father had seen her and he and his friends came swiftly to the rescue. Just as one of Squid's long arms touched Maliket to drag her into the sea, her father caught her and pulled her into his banca. Quickly the other fishermen attacked Giant Squid and drove him off. Soon Maliket was safely at home with her mother.

As for Maksil, he was so angry with Giant Squid because he had not brought Maliket back, that he punished him severely. "From now on," he commanded, "you must go to the shore at the risk of your life every year and bring me a young girl. One day I may find someone to take my daughter's place."

And that is why a whirlpool, said to be caused by Giant Squid's powerful arms, sucks a swimmer into its depths once every year.

At least, that is the story.

Retold by Rocio Dumaual
Illustrated by Eliseo Jose

How the Lizard Fought the Leopard

Once upon a time, in a certain forest, there lived a leopard.

One evening the leopard went out hunting as usual. He looked for a deer, or a pig, or even a small hare, but he found nothing, big or small. He was very hungry.

At last he met a lizard.

The leopard said: "You shall be my dinner tonight, Lizard."

The lizard said: "Sir, I am not big enough for your meal. Please let me go."

The leopard said: "No, I shall not let you go. A mouthful is better than nothing for a hungry person."

The lizard said: "I have no sharp teeth like you; I have no strong claws like you. You are strong and I am weak. The strong

47

should not kill the weak. It isn't fair. It is not the Dharma of our country."

The leopard said impatiently: "The weak always talk of the Dharma. The strong know only one law—'Might is right.' I have might; so I have the right to kill you."

The lizard said: "Very well, I am ready to die, but I'll die fighting."

At this the loepard laughed loudly. "I fight only with my equals," he roared.

"Very well," said the lizard, "give me three months and I'll be your equal."

The leopard agreed and they decided that they would meet again at that very place, at that very hour, when the three months were over.

Now the lizard began to get ready for the fight. Every day he went to the rice fields and rolled himself in the mud. Then he washed his face and hands and sat in the sun until the mud dried on his body. He did this daily for three months. Thus he became bigger and bigger and fatter and fatter, until he was a giant lizard.

At the end of three months, the leopard and the lizard met at the very same place, at the very same hour. The fight began. The leopard sprang forward and struck the lizard with his paw again and again. At each blow a cake of mud fell off the lizard's back, but the lizard was unhurt.

The lizard in turn jumped on the leopard's back and bit the leopard's ears and eyes and nose and forehead. He bit the leopard's body all over. Now the leopard was bleeding. Blood flowed from his ears and eyes and nose and forehead. Blood flowed from every part of his body. Still the lizard went on biting. The leopard's body was covered with wounds. He could not bear the pain

any longer. With a loud cry, he ran as fast as he could from the battlefield.

The poor defeated leopard sat under a tree. He looked over his right shoulder and felt it with his paw. There was a wound there. "That lizard bit me here," he moaned. He looked over his left shoulder and felt it with his paw. There was a wound there too. "And he bit me here," he groaned. With his paw he felt his ears, his eyes, nose, forehead, and back. There were wounds everywhere. He kept on repeating: "He bit me here, and he bit me here, and he bit me here. He bit me all over."

Now the leopard did not know that there was a woodcutter up in the tree. This man had seen the fight and heard the leopard's words and seen the leopard's wounds. He wanted to laugh. It

was such a funny sight—a huge leopard sitting under a tree and crying over the wounds caused by a small lizard! At last he could control himself no longer and he burst into a loud "Ha! Ha! Ha!"

The leopard looked up and saw the woodcutter. Had he been watched? He was angry because he didn't want anyone to know about his defeat. He climbed up the tree and snarled: "Stop your 'Ha! Ha! Ha!' or I'll eat you here and now."

"Oh, sir, please pardon me and spare my life!" implored the woodcutter.

"But you know my secret and for that reason you must die," roared the leopard.

"I swear by the gods of this forest that I'll keep the secret," said the woodcutter.

The leopard said: "That is not enough. You must swear by your wife that you won't tell her the secret. You must swear by your children that you won't tell them the secret." And the woodcutter swore by his wife and children. The leopard was still not satisfied. "What about the other villagers?" he said. "You might tell them."

"I swear by the Buddha that I won't tell the secret to anyone in the village," said the woodcutter. So the leopard allowed the man to go back to his village.

The leopard himself lay in his den, licking his wounds. He was still worried, for he thought: "These two-legged creatures are not to be trusted. I am sure that rascal the woodcutter will tell his wife the secret. When a woman knows a secret it is no longer a secret. I must go this very night and find out whether the man has kept his word." The leopard hurried to the back yard of the woodcutter's hut, crouched against the wall, and listened to the sounds in the house.

The woodcutter and his wife and their children were seated on a mat eating their dinner of rice and vegetables. Suddenly the woodcutter broke into peals of laughter.

"Father, why are you laughing?" asked the children.

"Sh-ssh. It's a secret," said their father.

"Father, please tell us the secret so that we can laugh too," begged his daughter.

"No! No! I must not tell it to anyone. I have sworn by the Buddha," replied her father.

The meal went on. Again the father began to laugh.

The woodcutter's wife said: "Children, your father must be mad. There, he has choked himself with his rice through laughing!" She slapped him hard on the back and held a cup of water to his mouth.

After dinner, the children went to their mats and were soon asleep. The woodcutter stretched himself on his rattan bed and his wife lay on her mat in the corner. But sleep did not come to the woodcutter or his wife. Every time he closed his eyes he felt he must laugh. His wife could not sleep either until she knew her husband's secret. Again the woodcutter went "Ha! Ha! Ha!"

The woman sat up on her mat. "What is it? Won't you tell me your secret now?" she asked. "The children are all asleep and no one will hear us."

The man said: "I have sworn to tell the secret to no one, not even to you."

However, the woman went on pleading until her husband gave

51

in. He told her how he had seen the fight between the leopard and the lizard and how the lizard had won. "Then," he said, "the leopard came to lie down under my tree and kept saying: 'That lizard bit me here! He bit me here! He bit me all over!'"

"Ha! Ha! Ha!" His wife joined in the laughter.

All this while the leopard had been crouching against the wall listening. He had heard the woodcutter's maddening "Ha! Ha! Ha!" and now he heard the woman's laughter as well. He was furious. He waited until the man and the woman fell asleep; then he leaped onto the roof of the hut. He removed part of the rice-straw thatch and slid into the loft. From there he lowered himself into the kitchen and opened the back door. Then he crept under the rattan bed, lifted it onto his back with the man still asleep, and walked out by the back door.

It was not until the leopard had reached the forest that the woodcutter awoke. He felt the bed moving. The moon had just risen and through the holes in the rattan bed he saw the black spots on the leopard's back. He knew that the leopard was out for his blood and he was terrified. Just then he caught sight of an overhanging branch of a big tree. In a flash he grasped it and lifted himself up into the tree.

Unaware of what was happening, the leopard went on. He reached the mouth of his den and put the bed down. But where was the rascally woodcutter? Grumbling, the leopard went back to look for him. There in the moonlight he saw the wood-cutter sitting in the tree. Without a word, the leopard dug his claws into the trunk and began to climb.

The woodcutter was very wide awake by this time. He shouted: "Mr. Leopard, if you love your life, climb no farther. There's a lizard just above me and he's wait-ing to bite you!"

Hearing the wood lizard, the terrified leopard leaped from the tree and ran away as fast as he could. In a moment he had disappeared from sight. And the woodcutter returned home still laughing "Ha! Ha! Ha!"

That was the last the woodcutter or anyone else saw of the leopard. They say he crossed the hills and hid his shame in a distant forest where there were no lizards or woodcutters.

Retold and translated by E. R. Eratne
Illustrated by Sumana Dissanayake